THE NIGHT BEFORE CHRISTMAS AT DUNDER MIFFLIN

THE NIGHT BEFORE CHRISTMAS AT DUNDER MIFFLIN

BRIAN BAUMGARTNER AND BEN SILVERMAN

ILLUSTRATIONS BY MAËL GOURMELEN

MARINER BOOKS

NEW YORK BOSTON

HarperCollins books may be purchased for educational, business, or sales promotional use. For information, please email the Special Markets Department at SPsales@harpercollins.com.

FIRST EDITION

DESIGNED BY Lucy Albanese
ILLUSTRATED BY Maël Gourmelen

Library of Congress Cataloging-in-Publication Data has been applied for.

ISBN 978-0-06-337272-6

24 25 26 27 26 TC 10 9 8 7 6 5 4 3 2 1

THE NIGHT BEFORE CHRISTMAS AT DUNDER MIFFLIN

'Twas the night before Christmas, and all through Dunder Mifflin
Not an accountant was stirring, not a mouse was a-clickin'.
Pam's painting was hung by reception with care,
And Stanley had filled in his last crossword square.

The holiday party was over
and Scranton's best employees
Were nestled all snug,
asleep at their PCs.

But as Kevin dreamed
blissfully of a full chili pot.

He awoke to a clatter down in the parking lot.

Away to the window he flew like a flash,
Oh no, he thought, Had Dwight's Trans Am crashed?
When he opened the blinds and looked into the night
Kevin's eyes were filled with an impossible sight.

There he saw Santa, dressed all in red,
And behind him, an elf, pulling a sled.
Santa tiptoed toward the building,
ordering the elf to move quickly.
"I can't," the elf hissed,
"Mose's shoes are too slippery."

Kevin sprang to his desk and pretended to snore,
As he secretly watched the pair bound through the door.

Santa reached into his sack and went straight to work
Delivering each employee their
end-of-year perk.

He started with Meredith,
empty bottles around her head,

He left aspirin for the morning,
which would be something to dread.

He left Andy a hat that read,
"I went to Cornell."

To Creed, he left air fresheners,
to mask his desk's strange smell.

Next to Pam, he placed a
brand-new paint set,

By Stanley, a retirement countdown, as if he'd ever forget!

For Oscar, a book of facts, for his
incessant corrections,

And self-tanner for Gabe and
his ghostly complexion.

For Phyllis, some yarn to knit a new mitten,
And to Ryan, an iPod, for Santa was smitten.

He slipped Jim a twenty and gave him a wink,
And the elf doodled on his forehead in permanent ink.

To Angela, pills to heal
her cat's infection,

And to Darryl a gold
watch inscribed "Dinkin Flicka" with affection.
He left a note to the warehouse, promising
Michael wouldn't enter for a year,

For Kelly, some headphones,
to watch videos so no one could hear.

To Erin, Santa's old George Foreman
Grill was bestowed,

While Toby was given garbage from the side of the road.

Santa then came toward Kevin, who kept his eyes shut tight,
And left brand-new drumsticks, to the accountant's delight.

SSKRRRRCH
NO SMOKING

When the gifts were arranged, Santa and the elf put up a tree,
But it burst through the ceiling, a sorry sight to see.
"It's too big!" cried the elf, shaking his head.
Santa stifled a laugh and whispered, "That's what she said!"

The two trimmed the tree with Dundies and beets,
Never noticing Kevin, pretending to sleep.

When his work was all done, Santa did flee
Giggling as he went with childlike glee.

Outside, he was happy, knowing he was the
World's Best Boss,
Taking care of his employees, whatever the cost.

Santa returned to the sleigh, pulled only by his elf,
And he began shouting in spite of himself:
"On Dasher, on Dancer, on Vixen, on Prancer!
On, Comet! On . . . Dwight! Can't you move any faster!?"

As the office began to awake from its slumber,
The employees looked around and
started to wonder.

They had no explanation
for the tree or each strange present,
And the foul stench of beets was
growing rather unpleasant.

Only Kevin knew the truth, he had seen it
all from his chair.
He called everyone to the window, and exclaimed,
"Look over there!"

They saw Santa down below, with a twinkle in his eyes.
Kevin couldn't believe his boss, Michael,
was missing the surprise.

Santa shouted to the window
as his sleigh inched
into flight,

"Merry Christmas to all—and to all a good night . . .

. . . except Toby."

ABOUT MARINER BOOKS

Mariner Books traces its beginnings to 1832 when William Ticknor cofounded the Old Corner Bookstore in Boston, from which he would run the legendary firm Ticknor and Fields, publisher of Ralph Waldo Emerson, Harriet Beecher Stowe, Nathaniel Hawthorne, and Henry David Thoreau. Following Ticknor's death, Henry Oscar Houghton acquired Ticknor and Fields and, in 1880, formed Houghton Mifflin, which later merged with venerable Harcourt Publishing to form Houghton Mifflin Harcourt. HarperCollins purchased HMH's trade publishing business in 2021 and reestablished their storied lists and editorial team under the name Mariner Books.

Uniting the legacies of Houghton Mifflin, Harcourt Brace, and Ticknor and Fields, Mariner Books continues one of the great traditions in American bookselling. Our imprints have introduced an incomparable roster of enduring classics, including Hawthorne's *The Scarlet Letter,* Thoreau's *Walden,* Willa Cather's *O Pioneers!,* Virginia Woolf's *To the Lighthouse,* W.E.B. Du Bois's *Black Reconstruction*, J.R.R. Tolkien's *The Lord of the Rings,* Carson McCullers's *The Heart Is a Lonely Hunter,* Ann Petry's *The Narrows,* George Orwell's *Animal Farm* and *Nineteen Eighty-Four,* Rachel Carson's *Silent Spring,* Margaret Walker's *Jubilee,* Italo Calvino's *Invisible Cities*, Alice Walker's *The Color Purple,* Margaret Atwood's *The Handmaid's Tale,* Tim O'Brien's *The Things They Carried,* Philip Roth's *The Plot Against America,* Jhumpa Lahiri's *Interpreter of Maladies,* and many others. Today Mariner Books remains proudly committed to the craft of fine publishing established nearly two centuries ago at the Old Corner Bookstore.